Beyond the Sands
Poems on Life, Love, and Nature

Jesus Diaz Llorico

Ukiyoto Publishing

All global publishing rights are held by

Ukiyoto Publishing

Published in 2023

Content Copyright © Jesus Diaz Llorico

ISBN 9789360167592

All rights reserved.
No part of this publication may be reproduced, transmitted, or stored in a retrieval system, in any form by any means, electronic, mechanical, photocopying, recording or otherwise, without the prior permission of the publisher.

The moral rights of the author have been asserted.

This is a work of fiction. Names, characters, businesses, places, events, locales, and incidents are either the products of the author's imagination or used in a fictitious manner. Any resemblance to actual persons, living or dead, or actual events is purely coincidental.

This book is sold subject to the condition that it shall not by way of trade or otherwise, be lent, resold, hired out or otherwise circulated, without the publisher's prior consent, in any form of binding or cover other than that in which it is published.

www.ukiyoto.com

Dedicated to my parents, Vicente Albaña Llorico and Amparo Dacutan Diaz Llorico whose love and support to me and my siblings, Bobby, Ma. Lourdes, Vicente Jr., Joan Frances, Paulette, Vicente III, and Michelle Jan have been immeasurable.

Acknowledgements

I give thanks to the following people:

To my wife, Annalie whose love and support has made this book possible.

To my sweet and loving daughter, Margaret Anjelie, thank you for helping me with compiling my poems and for encouraging me to submit my works.

To my son, Joseph James, thank you for supporting me all the way.

To my schoolmate, Ma. Asuncion Umali who encouraged me to write more poems when she read the first poem I posted on social media.

To my classmate, Susan Villamil whom I promised that if ever I publish a poetry book then her name will be included in. Though she passed away last May 2016, the promise is still fulfilled.

To my sister-in-law, Marivic Pasilbas and Jonalyn Adiong whose moral support gave me enough inspiration to write more poems.

Foreword

I have worked in the Middle East for more than twenty years and when I was assigned in an airbase, it was completely surrounded by the desert.

In the silence of the place, I was able to recall the life I had back home. From memories of my childhood and to the mischief of my teenage years, each memory was a grain of sand dripping down the lower bulb of an hour glass. Such bittersweet moments urged me to grab my pen and write lines to pay tribute to these memories.

Later on, I realized that the desert did not only bring nostalgia, but it also brought beauty and serenity. I appreciated nature and its resiliency against time.

This book is all about life, love, and nature. These poems are testaments that despite the sandstorms we encounter along the way, life goes on and remains to be a landscape in shades of gold.

Contents

The Dunes of Life	1
A Desert Life	2
Photos	4
The Garden	5
Rainbow	6
Old Woman	7
June 2013	9
Solitude	11
Moon	12
Leaf	13
Sandstorm	15
Grief (A Tribute)	16
Ode to A Dream	17
The Seed of Life	19
High School Reunion (NAMEI)	20
The Poet and The Moon	22
Storm	23
The Beauty of The Moon	24
The Desert Winds	25
The Stones	26
Dreams	27
Fire Call (Residential)	28
Forgotten Song	31
I Will Soon Be Forgotten	32
Internet Cafe (Circa 2013)	33
The Old Days	35
The Terrains Of Love	37
Clear Blue Sky	38
Forever in Love	39
The Mist of Love	41
Walk with Me	42
Our Dance	44
Sleep	45
We Dine	46
Every Spark	47
My Poems	48
One Fine Morning	49
A Few Seconds	50

Moonlight	51
One Cold Night	52
I Saw You	54
Ode to Beauty	55
Serenade	57
Simplest Poem	58
Song	60
Timeless Beauty	61
Valentine	62
Flower	63
Greater Love	64
In Our Time	65
What's in Your Heart?	66
You're Always There	67
First Taste of Love	68
Beautiful Girl	70

The Oasis   71

Alone (Haiku)	72
Branch (Haiku)	73
Clouds (Haiku)	74
Fear (Haiku)	75
Harmony (Haiku)	76
Leaves (Haiku)	77
Lost Love (Haiku)	78
Love Is Not Given (Haiku)	79
Moonlight (Haiku)	80
Rains (Haiku)	81
The Desert (Haiku)	82
The Moon Is Silent (Haiku)	83
The Sun (Haiku)	84
Walking (Haiku)	85
Life of An Old Man (Haiku)	86
After the Rains (Tanka)	87
Love Like A Leaf (Tanka)	88
Lovely Sunrise (Tanka)	89
Misfortune (Tanka)	90
New Leaves (Tanka)	91
Tell Her (Tanka)	92
Dry Leaf (Tanka)	93
Truth (Tanka)	94
Guimaras From Afar (Naani)	95

Hearts (Naani)	96
I See the Moon (Naani)	97
Moments of Love (Naani)	98
My World (Naani)	99
Rains (Naani)	100
Silence (Naani)	101
The Heart's Sting (Naani)	102
Heart (Crystalline)	103
Leaf (Crystalline)	104
The Withered Leaf (Crystalline)	105
Winds (Crystalline)	106

Beyond The Sand — 107

One Night in Abu Dhabi	108
Iloilo: The City of Love	109
Overlooking Guimaras At Night	110
September 2016 (UAE)	111
Yanbu, KSA	112
Zamora	113

About the Author — *114*

The Dunes of Life

A Desert Life

As I watch the sunset in this land
and the fading lights dims the desert sand--
a time my memory seems so right
to think of my loved one's out of sight

In the vastness of this ancient land
like flaming dots of red in the sand,
I miss the busy streets and city lights
and the traffic jams and those hurried lives.

I recall the years when I was young,
the party and the songs that were sung,
all the 'happenings' and so much fun
are now a memory and forever gone

I think of my family and friends,
a longing inside me that never ends.
Only in my mind, I get to be with them;
a sad empty feeling like a dream

The only thing that keeps me going
Is for my kids to finish their schooling.
Another ten years in the offing
to end my work and what I'm doing.

What I missed was my dad and mom.
I always need their comforting warmth.
For even when they've gone long ago.
Still, I'm not ready to let them go.

And sometimes when I cry at night,
I just wished that they hold me tight.
Their faces, constantly in my brain
and I just wept with so much pain.

I say now, if ever my time will come,
for twice, I'm near the end of my line.
I left a will to my dearest ones:
Please let me be laid beside my dad and mom.

Photos

As I look closely
at these photos,
what I see clearly
is faded youth.

For bright faces then
I used to see
but now a memory
Of past beauty.

These photos taken
are now retained
and never forgotten
in hearts forever.

As we slowly cling
to fading time,
these photos will bring
A silent story.

The Garden

In this garden I take a rest
to ease the sorrow in my chest
for I have seen so many years
before I felt these flowing tears.
The rains won't fall, the clouds are gone.
The winds and trees knew it is done
And in this garden where I lie
I let the sky gently pass me by.

Rainbow

I have created
a rainbow
just for you.
For in my dreams,
I see you.
When I'm awake,
I imagine you.
All because
of your exquisite
qualities
that is so beautiful
and lovely
that helps me through
in my lonely
existence here in
this country.

Old Woman

My heart is filled with strain and sympathy,
this picture that I never want to see,
a loose feeling borne out of misery,
when I looked on someone as frail as she.

As she calmly gazed the camera lens
beside the grass of the surrounding woods,
a somber scene in a secluded dense
for an old woman of mere livelihood.

Gloomy eyes with wrinkled hand and face
with a shred of cloth tied on her forehead
hanging gray hair in brow that interlace
wearing old garments cast in flowered beads.

While she gently holds a sickle in hand,
she slightly stooped on the weight of her back.
She holds firmly with a string as she stands
the bundle of sticks behind like a pack.

As I contemplate and looked more closely,
In her eyes, I saw a suffering heart.
This woman who was deprived of plenty.
To some, it's like life being torn apart.

It's not the load on her back that I see
but a life of pain and adversity.
The real truth that it can only be
a burden of poverty she carries.

As to our life's daily and constant strife
to this old woman born of tragedy
and who has no power to enjoy life.
To my God, I ask why this mystery?

June 2013

The heat is mild this month of June
as I rest in shade near my home.
While in silence, I heard a tune
of a bird's song this time of noon...

To me, how sweet this lovely scene,
a nature's grace to most unseen,
my feathered friends, true joy they bring
on this blithe sunny month of spring

They seek and peck and flap their wings
in quick glances, they eat and sing.
They flew above then play around
and hum their happy, chirping sound.

It seems they knew that I was there
as they flew near for me to hear.
I stood and gazed and hold my ground
and feel the beauty that abound

I think they call each other's name.
Maybe something about their games
Perhaps the food and other chores
Or their lovemates, they can't ignore

But their life was suddenly rouse
by a noise from a nearby house.
They flew away then out of sight,
left me enthralled, such a delight!

Alone again, and left behind
What had happened was kept in mind.
As to what I felt, what I saw
In my writings, I have to show

To my beauty, worth lavish praise
Whom I love in so many ways
This poem about the birds that flew
will be offered, again to you!

Solitude

The colors of the desert sand
transformed from the heat of the sun
and just a few species of trees
that gently sways in silent breeze
surviving from the harsh climate
of this barren and arid land.
I have learned to love its beauty,
the solitude that it gave me
as I waited for the pouring rain
in this dreary part of my terrain.

Moon

The moon grasped my heart tonight!
Like the glow of a burning lamp,
it gleams in a mantle of delight
beneath the clouds of misty damp

Like a wandering eye that glances
to every nook and corner streets,
a silent witness to life's romances
and all affairs most pure and sweet

My deep feelings drifted in the air
to the realm of the moon's domain
where its splendor of light will scatter
to her place where it will remain

On this night under the fainted stars
to the reddish moon that looks divine,
in sober reflections I humbly strive
that my muse conveys a modest sign,

As my heart refuses to rest tonight,
the moon exalts a greater mystery.
My continued toil of a worker's plight,
she eases the pain of melancholy...

Leaf

The stillness of the wind
is all around
as I walk along
this stretch of sand.

Oh! how I am amazed,
a beauty so grand
as I stood and gazed
at this majestic land.

I knelt and picked
a leaf in hand
and it was simply luck
that it's here I find.

As I stood and think
of her somewhere,
in this leaf, it sinks:
my true feelings for her.

If I can write truly
a poem in this leaf,
what a bonfire of poetry!
I can send lovingly.

As I turn around
and the leaf I threw,
it was left to the wind
and to nature's foe.

A leaf that brings
the really best in me
and in my heart, I knew
she's a past, but oh! so true...

Sandstorm

Oh! the howling of desert winds,
you are blowing so fierce again!
As you tried to restrain the minds
of tough camels and sturdy men

The clouds of dusts are on the roll
that raged across the plains and skies.
As it torments the wounded soul,
that pain was felt and blind the eyes

This desert boasts a mystic charm
and though it gives a ruthless howl,
men still endure with robust arms
deep in the vastness as they prowl.

To untamed winds that do not care
and dusts that billowed in the air.
The men and camels as they share
the sign that summer days are near.

Grief (A Tribute)

These aching hearts 'tis hard to keep
of life amidst so sudden, so swift
as thou hast gone in mournful sleep
That put us all in painful grief.

To God we seek for some relief
thy veins of love have flowed so deep
to dearest one in disbelief
even those not met has grieve and weep.

As each recall those lively youth
that whilst begun in younger years,
spent memories shed solemn truth
to thy righteous life, sweet souvenirs.

Now thou art asleep, released of pain.
To God we prayed with stricken hearts
Together in time, we'll meet again
To future where there's no need to part...

Ode to A Dream

A wishful thought of ardent past
Expect not I, my flame to last
This place I came long time ago
Amazed to find it's still on glow

The spark of love I used to see
Cheerful eyes, your look on me
Yet still in time, was kept in mind
how dear our life, we left behind

In all your touch, your love imparts
Left memories as we depart
The poems I hide, this desert land,
buried beneath the rocks and sand.

To me how swift these passing years
pursued we both, our own careers
as rains and dusts, and all the storms,
my heart, till now, does not transform.

Now, for once, in this midst of dream
I see you walking, all agleam.
The poems concealed, but still you see
and read it all, pure joy to me.

Neglect you seem, that I was near
but I was charmed it gave you cheer.
You held it close into your heart
and then you left and turned around

While I, this dream I tried to speak
to peace at last I plainly seek.
This throbbing conscious pain I see
To heaven, we're not meant to be...

The Seed of Life

"To dust men came and to this dust men shall return,"
a saying in the bible that has spawned like prey.
The seed of life that sown by men who never learned
a fortune that must never be squandered away

The desert is barren where water cannot dwell,
where trees grow in despair and miserable gloom.
The silent torment that rings like funeral bell.
A woman's value is determined from her womb.

As birds are free to fly and bees protect their queen,
their duty in life is to keep the breed alive,
a crowning achievement to see this wondrous scene:
The seed of humanity that men have to strive.

High School Reunion (NAMEI)

Reunions are like going back
to your original self:
the good old days,
reminiscing your past,
the times you spent in school.
Its cold and concrete walls,
the large windows and wooden floors,
where your everyday stay
was a struggle, a merriment
or just plain idleness
but it was where you flourished.
It was where soft, warm
and lovely friendships
are forever joined...
it was where first love,
puppy or passionate love
were equally created...
and the bridge in-between
the times in school and today
the gap in years, the distance
and the lack of communication--
that's what reunions are all about.
It's like feeling the sunrise
while watching the sunset
and celebrating as one...

It is a drawn measure
where success and popularity
of each member of the class
is different in many ways
and no matter what it takes,
it's still love and friendship
that connects this link
and brings forth these reunions.

The Poet and The Moon

What is a poet to the moon?
A poet is someone who hides
his tears in a secluded room,
one whose thoughts is so deep
that when he starts to write,
it's like the moonbeams flow
in the veins of his hand and mind
for the more pain he feels,
the lovelier his poems will be,
Oftentimes it's the readers who would say
he has a talent for poetry,
"wish he could write for us every day"
but in all simplicity
with the moon in all its glory,
it is saying to the poet
wish his heart will feel more pain
and his soul suffers every day,
so the readers could enjoy
a true and honest joy
that all his poems will be serene
until the last closing scene.

Storm

In my time, many years ago,
tt was always the same scenario:
that whenever there is a storm,
it's my favored time to stay at home
for I would listen to romantic songs
and dreamed and lay in bed all day long.

As to my favorite radio stations,
that at times I request for dedications
wherein today I do not know
if they're still on air or maybe no more.
The WIZ radio and D.W. double L.
and the familiar tunes...
'You are the minstrel and I'm your guitar'
The memory of 'the mellow touch',
words that I longed to hear again.

Those days are distant and seem forever
since I have become old and been away.
For nowadays, I always remember
the simple things, and the simple life
that makes me forget the everyday strife.
The beauty of living in my generation
as it gave me a chance to express
that period of my life where I was blessed
My days that I missed my life of long ago.

The Beauty of The Moon

My heart in silence wants to speak
to the moon that I longingly seek
for I want to tell her a story
about my love and past glory.

In her mute silence, she will listen
to tales of love and things I'm missing.
As I wrapped myself in her clouds
covered in bright and crimson shrouds.

As the wind changes course and rises,
my heart is filled with warm surprises.
And as I left this large ancient tree,
the moon keeps shining down on me.

My joy runs high as my heart swoons
from the rare beauty of the moon.
Like tokens around here small or big,
I'm just a piece of a broken twig.

The Desert Winds

The drifting clouds and desert winds
unlock the inner chords of my mind
as my eyes gazed the desolate dunes
this desert edge one cold afternoon.

A dream that I pondered for so long
and a wish that faded like a song,
the hope that she will come and enjoy
this hushed beauty of forgotten joy.

The rustling leaves at the top of trees
and the birds gliding in gentle breeze,
the swaying grass that is so profound,
love that in this hidden world I found.

As this opens my heart and my soul,
the enchanted wind that softly calls
to the passing of the clouds above,
I can feel the presence of her love.

The Stones

The stones...the marble stones,
it's the final resting place
after a tiring battle
in this weary world
of nameless moans…
no more laughter
no more tears...
and no one remembers
the last kiss
or the last embrace…
only the mysterious stars
in its never-ending lights
guards the stones
in its eternal peaceful rest.

Dreams

The stars seem to vanish in the skies
as I gazed into this lonely night.
For it's hard to see with wearied eyes
the blinking stardust of distant lights.

Alone I face this moonless night
and feel such longing
in my faraway shore
but as I see these scattered pebbles
and many tire tracks
on this deserted road
with the gentle swaying
of the nearby trees.
It's a wonder...
For everything in this moment of sadness
crumbles... and I just go on
with life and think of the dreams
of my loved ones back home.

This tender night of darkened skies,
regret is not a thing to be carried
For love is not deserts, trees, or poetry
But a sacrifice that one should aspire.

Fire Call (Residential)

It was dark... deep hours of the night
In a fire station along the street
With an ambience that seemed all right
as firemen plunged in peaceful sleep.
All at once, hotline sprung to life!
As everyone scrambled and leapt
In fire engines, in startled state,
they wore their firemen gears in haste.

With sirens wailing through the night,
fire trucks in glowing beacon lights.
Grim faced firemen stared in silence
as they neared the blazed so intense.
Radio burst its normal demand
from captain to the base command:
Disconnect, electrical source,
provide enough water supply.

A mixed feeling, hard to define
when responding to every call.
In hearts, they prayed to the Lord divine
for protection to guide them all.
As each, sized up the situation--
smoke, structure and wind direction

as people flee the fiery place,
it's where the firemen charged and raced.

As the entire crew arrived on scene,
the instructions came loud and clear,
three separate teams can be seen,
extinguishment, hit in front and rear.
With direct method of jet streams,
ventilation, smashing glass, windows
with axe, pike poles to tear down beams,
rescue the assigned team they knew.

They used forcible entry tools
to gain access, can be revealed
a dismay! as they saw weakened walls,
protective gears where their only shield.
They moved on and the search ensued.
Not a word, not a sound from each man.
Smoke filled residence they pursued.
To search for anyone, they can.

Each fireman has given their strength
So, the scene, be secured safely
an emergency of this length
where at stake could be family;
everything else are left behind.

They're no longer your son, brother
Husband, relative, nor a friend
But true fireman! like no other

Someone who really cares to know
what makes a fireman a fireman,
this calling was not easy to show.
The truth, they are the gentler ones
being exposed in hard situations.
Facing fears when there's fire around,
seeing nothing when smoke abound,
hearing repeated crackling sounds.

These men, simplest that you can find,
every news they're the silent ones
And when, urgency of any kind,
they are there to extend their hand.
Why they help strangers just like that,
simply in their hearts, a smile and
one call, they put life on the line
To me, this is what makes a fireman...

Forgotten Song

So hard to forget
so many moments
shared together,
so many places
to remember,
love that touched
my heart so long…
now a forgotten song.

I Will Soon Be Forgotten

There will be no accolades for me
in this life of tranquility.
And I will soon be forgotten
like winds that we cannot see.

As I stared in this space,
I think of how my adoration to poetry
turned into love,
That I belonged to it absolutely.
Sometimes...
the poems I rhymed is sketchy
and I always wait for you
to make it complete,
that if I think in the middle of the night
on the softness of your skin,
the delicate firmness of a kiss,
It will rouse me like sand dunes
and I'll find harmony
in the desert where my words exist.

If the connection has ceased
and our time finally end in peace,
yet the remains of my poetry
will be dedicated for you only.

Internet Cafe (Circa 2013)

The growth we get from this internet,
it lightens our load without much sweat.
This advantage is cheap and homely
that chatting with someone is now easy
and if you need to do some research,
you just type the word and click on 'search'.

So here I am! This internet cafe...
where faces I see seem so happy
but in all these moderate melee...
a beauty again! yes, I did see
and with all surprise and honesty,
she's browsing and reading my poetry!

Well, being caught in this situation,
she sprung into immediate action!
"Oh well, about these poems," she said,
"I don't know what's gone into his head.
who thinks he can impress his old flames!
This so-called nice poet named James."

"Better to play games," she further states,
"Where in each level I can relate
like this saga, pear and candy crush
where I enjoy, all these in a flash

even if this causes me headaches,
at least, it keeps me really awake! '

It is somewhat hard on what I've heard
and pretend that I was not bothered.
I just continued with my writings
and went on with my feeble readings,
but as she finished her fancy games,
She tapped my ear and said, "Hello James!"

"I love your poems and I'm just kidding.
This is just my own way of teasing.
You know, sometimes I like being funny
With you, I'm playing to be catty
for in my heart I really know and see
that all your poems are meant for me!"

The Old Days

They say the old days are better
and I think so too
but it was hard to communicate
and I know that this is true.
It does not make it any better
for the hearts and minds
of people of today and yesterday
has not changed at all.
It's only the gadgets and technology
that altered the lifestyle of people

Before we always feel the mild summers,
all the perfect sunshine days,
the rain in its endless drizzling,
that it was such a glorious feeling
especially if you're with friends strolling.
I used to walk to my friend's house,
have a nice conversation
the whole afternoon
and sometimes we drink
until we see the stagger of the moon.
Nowadays, people just go straight home
with their high-tech cellphones,
stay in their rooms,
and browse the internet all night long.

Now my days are part of history,
those happy times in life
where moments are shared
reflected and for me so sacred
and with the sunset
slowly creeping in the window of my flat.
It's time to prepare for my dinner
go out, take my nightly walk
and dream of the moon and wandering stars
for life will change again if I am gone.

The Terrains Of Love

Clear Blue Sky

Oh! It feels so nice to watch
this crystal-clear blue sky
as my heart seems up a notch
to see a view this high...

This moment I'd like to see
feeling refreshed anew,
A time I most want it be
to gaze this sky with you...

In dreams I hope you will come
so I can tell you why
Of how deep in love I am
with you, my dearest one...

As you look up in the sky
and if it makes you smile,
same I see here with my eyes
though far, a thousand miles!

Forever in Love

From the moment
I laid my eyes on you
that beautiful Monday
morning years ago,
I knew I already loved you
and I have loved you
from that moment on
until now.

Your smile, your kisses
and your voice has forever
become a part of me.
Your beauty lingers on
in my memory;
it's like soaring in the stars
and walking in the clouds
whenever I am with you.

After many, many years
of separation,
we finally meet again
and now that we are able
to talk again,
every day is always
the happiest day

in my life.

For when I say I love you,
I really mean what I say
for I'm telling you everything
down to the very little thing
my heart has to offer.
For you will always be loved
and will forever be mine
through time and eternity.

The Mist of Love

The mist of love
that flows in the air
is felt in the heart
that truly cares
and though only
a fleeting chance,
Still it was a great
and fine romance.
Our love was fragile
like the wind that blows,
streams of tenderness
on the river that flows
as quiet connection
was whispered softly
across the fields
and near the trees
yet this would come
to a sudden end
as doubts emerge
that cannot be mend
a time I most regret
this heart that I adore.
An aching reality that
our love is no more.

Walk with Me

An empty road.... this peaceful night....
As evening breeze blend with street lights.

Though far are we from city's glow
with only dunes and sands to show.

Come, be with me, my fairest one,
let us walk this road, hand in hand.

Then we will talk about the time
when we were young and in our prime.

The crescent moon up in the sky
will spread radiance for you and I

Tell me then, that moment arise,
first time we meet, love in our eyes!

While this divine and gentle wind,
just lightly brush your lovely skin

Whisper me then, the simple truth:
we're both in love since time of youth.

Our pleasant talk gaze from afar;
your sparkling smile mixes with the stars.

Together we'll laugh, have so much fun.
The world will know that we are one!

For you and I, this walk entails
It just seems like some fairy tale.

Though this dream, be out of the blue
I hope someday this will come true...

Our Dance

We danced…
your breath
grazing my chest
like in a pond
swirling…
so delicate
in every drop

we stood in silence
savoring the moment
hoping for it
to last forever

our I love you's
hangs in our eyes
and it clings…
your cheeks
finally
touching mine
and we're in a dream.

Sleep

As the night grew darker
and my dreams
got so much deeper,
the music and its mystery
started to engulf me.
As thick curtains of darkness
slowly covered my eyes
only the love songs...
your face looking at me
and your voice telling
sweet nothings
that I tried to understand
and those sweet laughter
like some mist in the clouds
I was trying to see.
As I went deeper into the abyss,
the night silently
took you away from me.

We Dine

We dine…
a special cuisine
and a glass of wine…
so delicious
sweet and hot.
we ate in silence,
you smile…
We look at each other
both aware
of the love passing through
the sweet corners of our eyes.
As my finger lightly taps
the edges of your glass
touching you…
like the tip of a leaf
savoring the dew
of the morning mist
it's a perpetual feeling
even without talking…
we're still in the world
of quiet heaven
and complete understanding.

Every Spark

Every spark,
every glitter
of the stars
that lights the night
is like a candle
at the edge
of my fingertips
burning
urging me to write,
my pen twisting
penetrating
into my dreams,
my spirit rising
breaking in silence
travelling
through the winds
that will lead
ultimately…
to the sweet chambers
of your heart.

My Poems

This desire to write
is from my heart
in this late of night,
you are a part.

For these silent hours,
the passions arise
and I was inspired
with joy in eyes.

The poems I made
are all for you
and just like I said,
my love is true.

One Fine Morning

It was a fine morning when she came,
my cherished passion and true flame.
A moment I can hardly wait
along this road and near the gate.
She walked in grace and flawless style
a breathtaking sight when she smiled.
That leaves were turned from brown to green
and fields of grass became serene.
Though it's not often that we meet
yet still our love remains so sweet.
With eyes that gazed over the skies,
my love that's far beyond the stars.
Though we spent many miles apart,
in life and love we are one heart.
That no matter how it will be,
she will forever be with me.

A Few Seconds

It was a scene I remember well
as we waited in school for the bell
You sat with friends in the hallway
talking and giggling all the way.

It started well with a simple stare,
a smile so sweet and full of care.
And it was a look that said it all
for it melted my heart and my soul.

Through years this shattered my mind.
In dreams, it was always in rewind.
These feelings that I deeply regret.
Love I never had, I can't forget.

If my prayers reach you o'er the sea
'Tis hope you recall so you can see
a few seconds between you and me
will forever stay in my memory...

Moonlight

The light that shines upon the door
and spreads fine glitters on the floor
comes from the beam of the moonlight
that slowly sweeps the cloudless night.
So, come my love, on this terrace.
Let us sit then and find our ways.
We will watch on the distant far
the bright full moon and falling stars.
As evening roses bloom in sight,
its stems gleaming from the moonlight.
Then we'll listen to soft music,
a tune that seems like a magic.
To heaven hosts we are entwined,
as we both know in hearts and mind.
This sweet touch of blithe harmony
binds our love to eternity.

One Cold Night

The cold full moon is out tonight
in this harsh winter away from home
as fainted stars hung in dreary sight
with all but gloom as he stood alone

The eerie silence of the winds
that gently blew the resting leaves
as it tears through his breath and skin
in grim stillness and chilly breeze.

Though no longer in prime of life,
his body has gradually declined
as tiredness is felt from torn and strife
after years of toil down the line.

His thoughts carried him to the past
of lifelong secrets and early love,
fond memories that will never last
that only the heavens knew above.

As the rays of moonlight calmly gleams,
there is one that blesses his soul,
a name spread along the moonbeams
who has quietly made him whole.

For years that they have been apart,
his hopes and dreams in silence sealed,
she remains the warmth of his heart
in teary times when thoughts are veiled.

As the evening falls in memory,
the moon now hidden from the clouds
As he walks away and silently
with the dark cold landscape left behind.

I Saw You

I saw you standing beside the tree
surrounded by lush of greenery,
a beauty that everyone would be
jealous to this pleasure that I see.
As gentle winds whisper tenderly
at nearby hills and through the valley,
the meadow glows as hearts befell
this stellar night that spread magic spell.
As my joyous heart sings to the moon
serenading with a soothing tune
with flowers, dreams and tender songs
and butterflies dancing all along
filled with praise and astounding passion
this flourish display of perfection
standing like a sweet flawless portrait
that transformed me to be a poet!

Ode to Beauty

One cherished look, no words inferred!
Thy beauty of such profound bliss
like soaring bird that must be heard
that longed to leave a lifelong kiss!
My happy eyes with utmost glee
as I secretly seek on thee.

Thy hair so silky, craved so much
endless artistry in thy smile.
A face most sweet, so fair to touch
the pose that swell! a grandiose style.
My lucky eyes have feast on thee
as I constantly want to see.

Though it seems, thou art like water
while I did grow immersed in fire!
Love ensures it does not matter
so long as both have famed desire.
My dreamy eyes have flown so free
as I certainly want to flee.

Destined to be, a world apart
but in the secrets of the night.
The thoughts of love do not depart
in minds and hearts both seems are right

My starry eyes...to heaven be
forever my heart will dwell on thee!

Serenade

I'm standing at your gate,
my fairest one
with a guitar while I wait
for you to come.

I will strum a lovely tune
so we can sing
under this radiant moon,
a charming thing!

As our blending harmonies
will fill the air,
we'll sing in your balcony
so nice to hear.

This unwavering serenade,
they all will know
that to God I always prayed
I love you so.

Simplest Poem

Tonight, as I write
the simplest poem
of my life…
with you sitting
on the porch.
Looking at you,
thinking of the
wonderful ways
you've done to me
as the winds
softly blow
the curtains
of our window,
my writings slowly
connived with the silent
twinkling of the stars.
the words spin
every syllable
echoing the love
between the earth
and the moon…
as you looked at me
and smile…
it was the
loveliest feeling

with the gentle
beating of our hearts,
you just turned
the skies and the night
to an absolute delight.

Song

As the sun gently leaves this desert plain
with wistful silence in the twilight air
and birds softly close their sweet refrain
as they firmly rest in their evening lair.

In the depths of this cloudy terrain
where the skies shed like a darken flame,
a distinct melody was heard again
to some distant houses where it came.

Unseen by all, behind these rusted walls,
my thoughts brought me to another world.
Her voice like a thousand stars that fall--
that kindles deeper than the twilight cold.

As profound images fill my mind,
it imparts a glow when I close my eyes.
The wind will blow and to her lips will find,
my tender kiss as I leave with a sigh.

Timeless Beauty

She smiles sweetly like morning light
as gentle winds and radiant sun
cast fragrance on this day of bright,
her cheerful eyes so full of fun.
Like drifting leaf on starry night,
a pleasing sight to everyone.
Her graceful charm a poetic write
of music and rhyme rolled in one.
In heaven bless for this famed chance
to gaze such beauty in our time.

Valentine

The way you sing
has dawned on me.
The lyrics it brings
just make me see
the sweet melodies
and it's all for me.

The way you show
has touched me so
as I looked into your eyes,
it really makes me sigh
your pretty face so divine
you are my true valentine.

Flower

Our life
is like a flower
How sweet it is
to know that
our scent
and beauty
will last forever.

Greater Love

Aside from the love of God,
is there a greater glory
than to have a woman's love?
A kind of story
where truth and dreams are all above
skies and hills,
trees and valleys?
Is there a more lasting memory
than seeing a smile so tender
and eyes of grace and glee?

I am just human
gifted with a soul to love a woman.
Winds and words,
harps and chords--
this is where hearts breeds love
gliding in clouds like a dove.
Keen and intense
that even in silence,
a love that was lost long ago
can be felt and still on glow.

In Our Time

If you are an unrequited love,
things would be different.
My dreams of you
would be like a fantasy
so beautiful
that it will stay in me forever,
but the problem is we're not
for in our time.
we have loved with so much love
that the love we had
as we both promised
will also end with so much love.

What's in Your Heart?

What's in your heart is all I ask
for I see in those clear brown eyes
a soft touch in my lonely heart
that has created a timeless art.

As bright stars filled the evening air
and winds gently kissed your sweet face,
a dream to behold as we stand
while I held you softly by the hand.

Years passed and times have changed
that things have gone way far too long,
why love remains we wonder why,
that it was seen in our lonely eyes.

There is something I can't forget:
your lovely smile and long dark hair.
As we listened to bygone songs,
it is where our hearts truly belong.

You're Always There

You're my ideal sunshine
that make my days so fine,
my star and guiding light
in my gentle walks at night,
that for every fantasy
you turned it into reality,
for you're always there
in such a beautiful way.

First Taste of Love

The first taste of love
is like the morning sunrise;
it changes everything.
The colors brighten
and the sound deepens
like little birds singing
an indescribable feeling
when I first saw you.

Those days in school
wearing your blue uniform,
your adorable smile
and your cute dimples.
the clip in your curly hair.
so sweet and wonderful
and to everyone in school,
you're the most beautiful.

That first exchanges
were made through friends
like normal teens
of what you like or not.
Why I do these things
or why I always drink
that eventually led

to scenes I don't want to be

Love can be heaven
or it can be a problem
but what is important
we became part
of each other's heart
through the passing of time.
You had always stayed
and will be in my heart forever.

Beautiful Girl

Beautiful girl,
beautiful girl,
you have such a lovely hair
for when I see you
coming down the stairs
you have caught me
unaware,

the way you smile,
the way you walk,
the way you sway your
silky hair
puts sweet perfume in the air
like the gentle autumn leaves
so nice to touch and weave.

The Oasis

(haikus, naanis, tankas and crystallines about nature)

Alone (Haiku)

I'm never alone
with books as my companion,
I'm always at home.

Branch (Haiku)

The withered branches,
broken rhythms of my heart,
does she care to know?

Clouds (Haiku)

The clouds passing by
carried my past in silence
to another time...

Fear (Haiku)

We still need to cross
this imaginary bridge
to conquer our fear.

Harmony (Haiku)

The birds' tenderness,
trees' reflection on water,
nature's harmony.

Leaves (Haiku)

The leaves' reflection
touched by moon in starlit skies,
thoughts of affection.

Lost Love (Haiku)

Lost love is still love;
there's no word to describe it,
only memories.

Love Is Not Given (Haiku)

Love is not given
to everyone by pure chance,
each has its own star.

Moonlight (Haiku)

The mystic moonlight
arouse unseen tenderness,
secrets of the night...

Rains (Haiku)

The continuous rains
dripping in my window panes--
thoughts of love so true!

The Desert (Haiku)

This immense desert,
keeper of my sweetest dreams;
the stars make it glow.

The Moon Is Silent (Haiku)

The moon is silent,
so cold, yet its influence
is all around us.

The Sun (Haiku)

The sun going down
brings the last breeze of the blue,
birds in hurried flight.

Walking (Haiku)

A night full of stars,
an old road draped in moonlight,
and a little tune.

Life of An Old Man (Haiku)

So lonely down here
disconnected and alone;
life of an old man.

After the Rains (Tanka)

Right after the rains
such different worlds arise
shaping fantasies
far beyond one's dreams and thoughts,
true reflection from the skies.

Love Like A Leaf (Tanka)

Our love's like a leaf
being soaked by the soft rain
until one forgets
that from steady showering,
no one can see its weeping.

Lovely Sunrise (Tanka)

A lovely sunrise
for it's like a sparkling gold
in the sea of glass
with the flight of birds singing
and leaves rustling in the trees.

Misfortune (Tanka)

Every misfortune
we met in this frenzied life
is always flavored
with an exquisite lesson
of learning and experience.

New Leaves (Tanka)

Those little new leaves
unfamiliar with the rains
learns from every drop
a life of comfort and pain
above the quiet tree top.

Tell Her (Tanka)

Tell her what you feel
for many do not express
their real feelings
once opportunity's lost,
it's a lifetime of regret.

Dry Leaf (Tanka)

The dry leaf that flies
now lain forever in time
between earth and sky...
and seeing with my silent eyes
where its spent life softly lies.

Truth (Tanka)

When the truth sets in,
there is almost no escape
with two options left:
that is to face them squarely
or build a fantasy wall.

Guimaras From Afar (Naani)

The bright mountain greens
with sparkling sea in between
and its hills holding through
in skies of white and blue.

Hearts (Naani)

Do hearts have options
when love comes to play?
For we can't decide who to choose
as love takes it all away.

I See the Moon (Naani)

As I see the moon,
its light so old and drawn
faded youth and tender heart
awakes the poetry inside.

Moments of Love (Naani)

When our eyes meet
with same heartbeat,
our speech would only spoil the essence
of perfect harmony....

My World (Naani)

I walk in this heat
on this busy street.
My world suddenly stops in delight
when I saw you in sight!

Rains (Naani)

These incessant rains
on my window panes
as it keeps pouring on the wall;
memories of our love that fall...

Silence (Naani)

When quiet tears are shed
and never a word was said
the depth of silence
are like the moon and stars.

The Heart's Sting (Naani)

If a heart wants something,
it's hard to stop its sting
for it will pour like rain
even the mind tried in vain.

Heart (Crystalline)

My heart wants to be where you are
for your love kindles like a bright star.

Leaf (Crystalline)

The withered leaf kept in my book,
a witness to love long lost in time.

The Withered Leaf (Crystalline)

The withered leaf left in the ground,
a witness to love long lost in time.

Winds (Crystalline)

The wind comes like music this dark night;
it heals my soul and hearts' desire.

Beyond The Sand

One Night in Abu Dhabi

My heart seems to know
to see these buildings glow
for in this place years ago
a desert archipelago,
in its valleys and natural sands
Bedouins roam this ancient land
playing lyres and piping songs
beneath the stars all night long,
harping their sweet serenade
as they rest under the oasis shade
and with moon in-between their hearts
a forgotten era of timeless art.

Iloilo: The City of Love

Iloilo is the city of love
in the province of smile
that it's nice to be a part of
a place for simple lifestyle

a walk along Fort San Pedro
with a view of the lovely sea
overlooking the isle of Guimaras
where one sees are green and lush.

Listening to an old love song
that stayed in heart for so long,
a stroll that makes one recall,
a love that broke and fall.

Iloilo being the city of love,
it's beauty so far above
remembering the time with you,
this place we call Fort San Pedro.

Overlooking Guimaras At Night

Tonight, as I walked in gentle breeze
all alone with my spirits high
with leaves swaying from sturdy trees
and flames of stars hung in distant sky

that something strange happened to me
it seems I was carried to the sea
as it unfolds in front of me
the ideal things I longed to see

mountains and trees and all its beauty
seas and clouds in heavenly glory,
these are the things that makes one happy
to see these as part of their story.

September 2016 (UAE)

This place beams from the heat of the sun
as birds hide in shadows one by one
for even the few passing clouds
leisurely moves from this draping shroud.

but soft winds hang in the open
as leaves gently sways in nearby trees,
a sign that summer will be broken
and signals the coming of winter breeze.

Yanbu, KSA

As I walked along this road
this street called Ishara Al Lutfi,
seeing people silently walking
not minding anyone they're seeing.

As grasses of summer is swaying
from the hot desert winds,
their pointed tips seem glowing
from the sun's fiery binds.

Though a little bit troubling,
its leaves slowly diminishing
but all this has to happened
in life cycle as we imagined.

As life here is sad and limited,
this street called Ishara Al Lutfi,
my simple walk will just be part
of another man's forgotten history.

Zamora

As I walked along this street
I feel the silence around
with dogs roaming aimlessly
and trees with such dark leaves
moving silently from soft winds.
The moon is covered by
dark clouds matching
the formation of flickering stars
scattered in the skies.
I can see my shadows
beneath the damp lamp posts
and dark reflection
from the few watery pools
along the pavements
with my stress slowly
diminishing from my walk.
I say to myself,
"Enough of this sentiment
for I am now
in front of my home."

About the Author

Jesus Diaz Llorico

Jesus Llorico is a retired Fire Captain. He has risen to the ranks: a firefighter, driver operator, crew chief, fire lieutenant, fire captain, and training officer. He was an Overseas Filipino Worker as he had spent more than two decades of service in the Middle East.

He is the second of eight children. He has been married for 28 years to his wife and they have two children together.

Having spent over two decades working in the Middle East, he was often assigned in areas where he could appreciate the beauty of nature. The peaceful scenery of the blue sky and the quiet desert made him discover the beauty in solitude and the poetry in nostalgia.

www.ingramcontent.com/pod-product-compliance
Lightning Source LLC
LaVergne TN
LVHW041853070526
838199LV00045BB/1575